STECK-VAUGHN

PAIR-IT BOOKS

Let's Be Friends

Written by Michael K. Smith

STECK-VAUGHN
COMPANY

A Division of Harcourt Brace & Company

Friends swim together.

Friends dress up together.

Friends paint together.

Friends laugh together.

Friends read together.

Friends dance together.

Friends like each other.